All For Nothing

Joe Mannherz

Copyright 2022 by Joe Mannherz

All rights reserved.

Published by Mannherz Music LLC

Library of Congress Cataloguing-in-Publication date available

ISBN: 979-8-9876703-0-9

This book is a work of fiction. Names, characters, places, and incidents are either the product of the author's imagination or are used fictitiously, and any resemblance to actual persons, living or dead, business establishments, events, or locales is entirely coincidental.

Table of Contents

For my Parents
and their Unconditional Love

PROLOGUE

"Go figure." It's an expression used by a new generation of people to explain away what they don't understand or can't comprehend. When they can't "divine" solutions to their problems, the expression flows freely from their mouths like water from an unclosed, open-ended faucet. As though the mere utterance of said phrase justifies their ignorance and they can put their predicament away like ill-fitting old clothes in a box, stored in the Attic, never to be thought of again. Problem solved. In my line of work as a private investigator, I can neither afford to use the expression nor fail to solve problematic situations that confront me. If I did, I would be labeled a modern neophyte and find myself quickly out of a job.

This is the story of one of those situations. One of those, "predicaments."

This is the story of a very special, extremely sought-after diamond affectionately nicknamed "Nothing." Not because it was unsubstantial or worthless, on the contrary, it was because it had no external blemishes or internal flaws whatsoever; was as transparent as a layer of cellophane floating on water and next to priceless.

And it was missing.

In the beginning, the solution to said disappearance appeared "crystal clear" and relatively simple. In the end, it was perplexingly opaque and almost cost me everything.

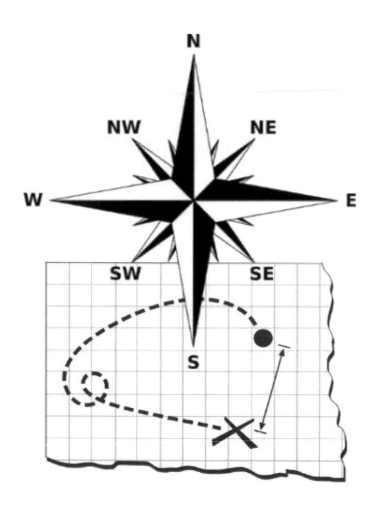

CHAPTER 1
It all has to start, Somewhere

To begin imparting this adventure to you by saying "In the beginning, God created the heavens and the Earth" would appear a tad melodramatic and would contain information not relevant to this story. Not to mention raising plausible deniability regarding facts as far as my memory is concerned. Let us just borrow a quote from Julie Andrews who succinctly stated, "let's start at the very beginning" and leave it at that. Note to reader: Anyone who mentally sang that phrase while reading it is, in my opinion, well versed. Pun intended.

My brother Mark, who would be described as a tall, introverted, self-proclaimed philosopher, mild mannered "Baby Huey" type of individual is 9 years my junior. He began his vocation in a monastery studying to be a Franciscan priest, which is, interesting enough but neither relevant nor germane to the story. Moving forward as they say, he realized after several years of study that their idea and his idea of how to serve the Lord differed in many respects by several degrees, so he left. He subsequently turned to his avocation in music and established what would later become a very lucrative recording company. It is there that the real story begins. I, the elder of we two on the other hand, who would like to be described as the rugged handsome type; pseudo intellectual extravert, would, by many individuals, refer to me as "average." My parents and close relatives all worked for the local telephone company, so naturally, I chose a career in law enforcement which led me inexplicably to become a Private Investigator. Follow the connection? Pun intended. Again.

Because of my own involvement with music from a young tender age i.e., piano lessons, church choirs, garage bands, you name it, my brother recruited me to help him write several novel songs he had in mind. After many brainstorming sessions and countless hours of rehearsing, we came up with, what one would call a 'palatable song.' And on a warm day in late June in the summer of 1989, we recorded a demo of that song which, for all intents and purposes, was not to be released as is, but would somehow make its way to the public and cost me not only the life of my brother, but nearly the love of my life as well. By now, you're asking yourselves, how did the writing of a song and the disappearance of a diamond cause, individually or collectively, so much misery?

Me too.

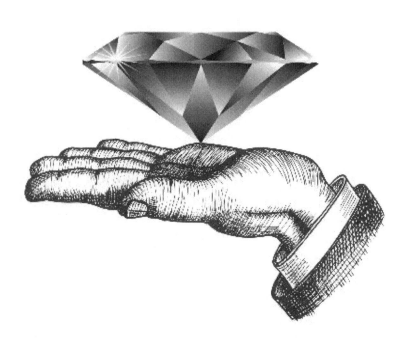

Chapter 2

Speaking of Diamonds

Diamonds, as you are aware or should be, come into being deep within the bowels of the earth when carbon formations are subjected to extreme pressures. The value of said diamonds is the result of a combination of the assessment of their four C's i.e., clarity, color, cut and carat weight. The "Nothings" 4C ratings were off the chart. Beginning its life in South Africa some 2 billion years ago, then extracted from the ground via open pit mining and blasting techniques, the diamond found its way to the United States via the back roads and alleys of Cape Town, Istanbul, and China. To say it was a short trip would be an understatement. But shorter relatively speaking than how long it took to make. Obviously. Released for sale from the De Beers Consolidated Mining Company, the largest mining and distribution facility of diamonds in the world, the diamond was finally brought to auction by Sotheby's at their Hong Kong location. Sotheby's is a British founded American multinational corporation with headquarters in New York City. It is one of the world's largest brokers of fine art and decorative jewelry and has 80 locations in more than 40 countries. But it is from their Hong Kong location, the city many refer to as the 'Gem of the Orient' where its diamond trade is most robust.

Just before the commencement of the auction, a well-dressed, elderly man in his mid to late seventy's approached the auctioneer. Ambulating quite slowly, due to what appeared to be an arthritic condition of his lower extremities, he had a determined bearing and confident stride to his gait. Those who saw him looked quickly away. Those who were in his direct line of travel found themselves moving obliquely out of his way. He neither varied direction nor looked askance from the path which led him directly to the podium.

"Who oversees this auction?" inquired the patron in a thick Russian accent.

"Why Mr. Feder's" replied the auctioneer.

"Tell him, I would like to have a word with him before the auction begins" exclaimed the Russian.

"Whom should I say is requesting his presence" asked the auctioneer.

To this question, the elderly gentleman held out an aged hand holding a circular metallic pendant upon which bore the likeness of Stalin with the sickle, hammer and star of Mother Russia embossed upon a gold background.

"Tell him, I'll meet him in room 204 on the second floor in ten minutes" proclaimed the gruff voice. Whereupon uttering this statement, the gentleman turned and walked out of the room as stately and determined as he had entered. And, to the same crowd response.

Ten minutes later, the door to room 204 opened to admit a tall lanky individual that one could only describe as Arthur Treachers' double.

"You're not supposed to be here" the 'Treacher' clone exclaimed.

"If anyone sees you, we'll all be in trouble. And the consequences of which I would not like to think about."
"Do not fret yourself. I took all the necessary precautions to remain incognito" stated the elderly gentleman.

"But if you were seen, we could. . ." began Mr. Feder.

"Shut up," said the Russian, "we don't have time for this right now. You have a particular piece of merchandise coming up later in the auction that I need you to pay very close attention to and follow these instructions to the letter." Upon making this statement, the aged Russian placed a piece of paper into Mr. Feder's hands.

"You will act upon these instructions to the letter is that understood?" said the Russian.

A solemn and slow nod was Mr. Feder's only response.

In the rear of the auction room two floors below, stood an attractive petite' Euro-Asian woman looking decidedly nervous and deliberately seeking the shadows of the chamber. As fashionably dressed and becoming as she was, that fact alone was making it harder for her to seek and find anonymity. She also found herself more anxious than she wanted to be at the end of an unusual half-hour delay in the normal proceedings. The auction, not yet having formally begun, saw a goodly amount of people slowly making their way to their seats. Among them was a man whose manner and dress did not proclaim him to be a regular auction attendee. This fact was not only obvious to the other patrons but the auctioneer and lady of mystery as well. Uncomely and taller than most of the Hong Kong patrons attending the auction, it was obvious that he was not a native to this part of the world, or to auction protocols in particular. He was manipulating the auction manifest as a non-bookie would fumble his way through a racing form. He was also observed to engage in rapid and numerous disjointed conversations with his fellow patrons about said form. His erratic behavior was subdued only by the arrival of the auctioneer. The auction gavel, having been struck three times, produced the rapid cessation of cacophony as it was intended. The subsequent silence only served to heighten the anticipated mood of our lady of mystery. The auction began and proceeded through the sale of several items without much ado from anyone. It wasn't until item fourteen arrived on the auction billet that produced a noticeable visual and audio change to the dynamics of the room.

Papers crumpled, feet and buttocks alike shuffled nervously in mark time. Conversations, both anxious and muted could be heard escalating throughout the room. After several minutes of the rooms heightened state, a side door opened to the chamber and a man carrying a small ornate box strode into their midst. Silence ensued. The man reverently placed the box upon a pedestal next to the auctioneer and silently withdrew. The auctioneer, apparently nervous, opened the box to reveal a small-bagged object in blue velvet secured with a gold cord. With shaking fingers, the auctioneer untied the bag and uncovered a white diamond. This reveal brought an audible gasp from those in attendance as a single tear cascaded down the cheek of Our Lady in shadows.

"Next item up for bid" stated the auctioneer, "is a white diamond from Cape Town South Africa being sold by the De Beers company through Sotheby's of a 62.2 carat GIA graded stone affectionately named, 'Nothing.'" Audible intakes of air could be heard resounding throughout the chamber.

"Opening bids will begin at $50 million", stated the auctioneer, "do I hear $50 M?" For a moment, no one moved. Everyone appeared suspended in space and time. Then, ever so slowly, one by one, auction paddles began to rise. And they continued to do so until the stranger raised his own paddle at the announced $62 million mark. At which time, no one else followed suit. And it remained that way for several minutes. Not unusual at an auction of this caliber, but as the seconds ticked by and there were no other paddles raised or telephone calls answered, the suspense increased. Even more alarming was the bid at which the proceedings stalled. Even though $62 million is by anyone's standard a lot of money, it is not exceptionally high for this type of diamond. The largest diamond auctioned prior to this date was known to the diamond world as the "Pink Star." GIA graded at 59.6 carrots it sold at auction for $71.2 million. The 'Nothing' was much larger, graded much higher and was apparently selling for much less. Something was amiss.

And the situation was of particular interest to our mysterious lady. The auctioneer seemed nonplussed by this conundrum and preceded in his usual auctioneer verbiage: "$62 million going once, going twice, sold for $62 million." At this pronouncement, the room became unconstrained. People were waylaying around obviously not knowing what to do with themselves or their compatriots. The tall gangly stranger who bid last slowly made his way up to the podium to exchange words with the auctioneer. The elderly Russian gentleman, who had been observing the proceedings from the boxed seats on the second floor, smiled as he stood while mumbling to his associates who surrounded him, "kak I dolzhno byt'" (as it should be). Pausing only briefly to be assisted with the donning of his coat, both he and his entourage left as unobserved as they had entered. On the auction floor itself, the lady was nowhere to be seen.

Chapter 3
The Trip Home

The whole experience was just surreal. It was something he had never done before in a place he had never been before. And he hoped, while he was getting his boarding passes analyzed by flight security, that he'd never have to go there or do that again. If someone would have told him yesterday that he would be purchasing anything of the nature, quality, or extravagant value of the item he just procured, he would have told them they were crazy. But people have a way of being persuaded to do things they would not normally do, especially if your life is being threatened. And he was absolutely convinced that indeed, his life was being threatened. He watched too many television shows as a kid not to recognize the bad men in the black trench coats. So, when they showed up at his studio the other day and made the proposal that put him on the airplane to Hong Kong, he knew he didn't have a choice not to go. He knew five years ago that when he borrowed the money he needed from less than scrupulous sources, a day of reckoning such as this would be forthcoming. But overall, the trip wasn't so bad. He did exactly what they instructed him to do; went to the location they told him to go, did exactly what they told him to do at said location and now he was coming home.

No harm; no foul, right? So why did he feel that he had broken every law and moral code known to mankind? Why did he feel that everyone was watching him?

Well, maybe not everyone. Just someone.

Chapter 4
A House is a Home

I live in the house I grew up in and share it with my brother Mark. We didn't plan it that way, it just sort of happened. Our sisters married, moved away, and had families of their own. Mark and I stayed single. When our parents died and the house fell into their estate, I just couldn't bring myself to sell it. Mark, who was living out of state at the time, came back to open his recording studio and didn't have anywhere to live. The house was too big for one person, so we decided to share it. He occupies the basement and half of the first floor, and I the other half and the upper stories. We share the kitchen. We usually don't get in each other's way because he works most days at the recording studio, and I do most of my sleuthing at night. He needs his clients to be attentive and focused whereas I need mine to be more susceptible and compliant.

I grew up in the northeast corner of Baltimore City. Far enough out of town to feel rural but close enough to the heart of the city to be urban. This made commuting to cultural events and the inner harbor area easily accessible by car or bus and it was a good stretch of the legs if you felt energetic. I lived with my parents, my brother and our two sisters in a house one would say 'just about fit' the six of us. During the day, when everyone else was 'out and about,' and you were home, the house was comfortable.

But in the evening when everyone was home, it felt a little claustrophobic. There were only three bedrooms. My parents occupied one, my sisters the second and my brother and I the third. And we're not talking about large bedrooms either. 8' x 10' or 10' x 12' at the most.

Naturally, my brother and I were forced to take the smallest of the bedrooms because we were "boys," and by some unwritten rule we didn't need that much space. That may well be true if two people are standing in the room. But at night, when one must sleep, two boys measuring length wise, along with various pieces of furniture, mathematically can't fit in an 8' x 10' room. This dilemma must have been prevalent in households outside of our own because some ingenious person solved this problem by inventing the "bunk bed." If you're unfamiliar with that term, let me elaborate. It's two beds stacked on top of each other, connected at the four bedposts in a mortise and tenon fashion. It was conveniently equipped with a ladder so one could easily egress to and from the upper bed as well as an upper bed railing to protect its occupant from accidentally rolling over in the middle of the night and falling to the floor. This significant 1" X 4" piece of pinewood, stretched from the top of the bed, where it's undercut "U" shape sat over the headboard, to the bottom of the bed where it's opposite end just sat precariously on top of the footboard. I wanted to describe this piece of apparatus to you because whoever invented the ingenious "bunk bed" didn't spend enough time and forethought in the design of the "safety rail." And I use that term as an oxymoron. It may have been a railing, but it surely wasn't safe. Point of fact. As I mentioned previously, I am Mark's older brother by nine years. Meaning, when I was ten years of age, Mark was just a baby. By way of physical differences therefore, he was granted the use of the bottom bed. This made sense because he couldn't possibly climb up to the top bunk. "Duh!"

I personally didn't mind it whatsoever. From that vantage point, I could look out the window just behind the headboard and down two stories into the illuminated back alley, where I could keep a watchful eye on "my turf." I was perfectly content with those sleeping arrangements until one fateful night when I became ill. It developed from a stomach virus which overcame me while I was sleeping. As the condition worsened, it caused me to thrash about in my sleep. During this "thrashing phase," I happen to wedge my legs under said "safety railing" dislodging it and sending it crashing to the floor. If you've never heard the term "ungodly noise" before, you are about to have it explained to you. Imagine, if you will, a sound that not even God could tolerate. Think about it for a minute. Upon its descent to the floor, the bed railing would not be considerate or courteous enough to your ears to hit just once and make one sound. Oh no! Because it was dislodged one corner at a time, it struck the floor one corner at a time. And did I mention we had hardwood floors? Keep that in mind. If you ever had the occasion to witness a spinning coin or a Tumbler glass decelerating from its spin, you will remember that it does so very awkwardly while wobbling quite a bit. And I'm sure you can mentally hear the noise that it makes while doing so. Now, imagine if you will, a seven-foot-long piece of softwood dropping approximately six feet; hitting one end at a time, in succession, on a hardwood floor 'continuously,' until it eventually decelerates and wobbles no more. At three o'clock in the morning, when there is not even a bird chirping, this "ungodly" sound would be enough to wake the dead. But did it wake me? Hell NO! I was still thrashing about in the throes of stomach flu. The only thing that woke me was throwing up during the freefall down to the floor following the trajectory of the bed railing. I conveniently was wide awake to feel the impact of my back and head on the bed railing while my face was being simultaneously treated to the vomit which followed me down. By now, you must be asking yourself, "if you didn't wake up when the railing hit the floor, how do you know what it sounded like?" Did I mention this scenario repeated multiple times throughout my childhood? Fortunately, on most of those occasions, I didn't follow the bed rail down to the floor. But I sure did wake up startled by the noise it made. And it was on one of those occasions that I saved my brother's life.

As the years went by, as they normally do, and we got older, as we normally do, I grew too big to sleep on the top bunk. My weight was such that I was overpowering the bed springs to where they were almost touching my brother sleeping in the bottom bed. Not to say that I was anywhere near being a fat child, but that the bedsprings were not that powerful. By comparison, my brother was a lightweight. He now was at the age where he could climb up to the top bunk, and he bugged my parents continuously to do so until they relented. As is true in most cases, history unfortunately repeats itself. Did I mention the ungodly three a.m. bedrail noise is much louder when sleeping on the bottom bunk? Well, IT IS! And when heard often enough, one acclimates to become wide awake at the very first strike of the bed rail to the floor. It was on a night such as this when I was startled awake by the noise of that first bed rail strike. What surprised me, however, was the appearance of a secondary shadow which followed the bed rail. I'm still astonished to this day as to how fast my semi-comatose mind reacted to this illogical situation. It deduced, rather quickly, that if the first shadow was the bed rail, the second shadow had to be my brother. Disregarding any thoughts for my own safety, my athletically trained body reacted quick enough to catch my brother before he hit the floor and died.

The only reason I'm relaying these childhood stories to you at this time, is so that you can have a keener insight into why I devoted my life to law enforcement. I attribute it to the combination of the multiple head injuries I sustained falling six feet from my upper bunk, as well as the elation which overcame me upon saving my brother's life. These experiences instilled in me the determination and sense of purpose to track down and prosecute, if need be, the inventor of the 'bunk bed' and so-called 'safety rail.'

As we matured, we acquired tastes for different things and chose different professions. Our common denominator was always music. And, one other thing; baseball. Collectively, between the two of us, we had more baseball cards than anybody on earth. That's the way it seemed to me anyhow. Our one big "tiff" was arguing over who was the greatest home run hitter of all time. He claims it was Hank Aaron. Even though he admits Barry Bonds hit more "total" home runs, he still likes Hank Aaron better. I always argue that he doesn't take into account the modern era's extended season, therefore the proportional number of regulation games played today versus those in the "good old days." In the end, he has his hero and I have mine. We agreed to disagree. Nowadays, when the house gets a little claustrophobic for the both of us, and we have some 'free time' on our hands, we head down to my brother's recording studio. There, we either dabble in a little collaborative music writing, mix other people's soundtracks, or shoot a mean game of pool. My brother had the pool table installed to keep his clients calm and collected during their frequent infighting over disagreements concerning their music.

"You remember the Dillon brothers?" he asked me one day in the middle of a game.

"I sure do" I responded.

"Didn't one stab the other over a disagreement about who was going to sing the verse and who was going to sing the chorus to one of their songs?" I asked.

"You got that right" he said, "and you should have seen them during their recording sessions. You would think they weren't related at all. And their frequent 'combat sessions' nearly destroyed the studio."

"Isn't that what the pool table was for?" I asked, patting the felt.

"No!" he replied, "that's what this was for" where upon he reached under the pool table and to my surprise, pulled out a shotgun.

"Wow, that's a beauty" I said, "can I see it?"

"Sure" he said while handing me a pristine, Remington 870, The King of American shotguns. After careful scrutiny, I handed it back.

"When billiards didn't suffice to keep the peace," he exclaimed while putting the gun away, "this puppy always worked."

"You're the man" I said. And he is.

Chapter 5

Sam Spade I'm not

I work out of a small office in downtown Baltimore on the first floor of what once was an old savings and loan building. It's nothing fancy by any stretch of the imagination but has all the modern conveniences for me to adequately perform my duties as a private investigator. Equipped with fax machines and telephones, to communicate with the outside world, to computers and miles of filing cabinets to collect and store information. And Doris, my secretary, who always reminds me of Anne Southern, the actress who played Susie McNamara in CBS's "Private Secretary" which ran on television in the late 50's. Doris and I met a few years ago when she was one of my clients. She was involved in a personal relationship that was stagnant and uninspiring, with a man who was neither loving nor supportive. In fact, he was abusive to her, and she was eager to sever their relationship before it became detrimental to her health, literally. In my usual flamboyant nature, I strongly persuaded her partner that it would be in his best interest to dissolve their 'relationship' and relocate himself elsewhere while he was still physically capable. It was just by happenstance that at the end of our business dealings, I was in need of a competent and reliable secretary, and she needed a job. Doris and I have been together ever since.

I'm there to make sure she's gainfully employed and she's there to make sure that everything runs smoothly, including my life. The latter, she pays particular attention to and appears to devote much of her time, to my bewildered amazement and my everlasting gratitude. Oh, and I also forgot to mention my private live-in-tenant, "Babe." Babe is an 8-ft, 6-in Indian cobra who resides in my inner office. I'm not, by any means, one who you would call a "reptile person." I'm more of a Bernese Mountain dog kind of guy. But the snake was given to me by an affluent Indian client I worked for some time ago as partial payment for helping him settle a family inheritance dispute. His financial payment was more than adequate to cover my services, but he felt "obligated" to extend his gratitude by giving to me one of his pet cobras. It's a member of a rare variety of one of the only non-poisonous cobras still in existence in India. Who was I to say "no?" And, as it turned out, the snake is great company. It doesn't talk much and agrees with everything I have to say, it keeps all my clients civil during our discussions, and the office free of rodents in her spare time. During the times that my inner office isn't being used, naturally, I would let Babe out of her enclosed aquarium to 'stretch her legs' so to speak, where she then performs the latter of her office duties. You don't want me to tell you what happened the last time I forgot to close the inner office door during one of Babes stretch breaks. Why the name "Babe"? Her previous owner called her that, and who am I to disagree with "by what name" a snake wants to be called?

Things being the way they are in downtown Baltimore; parking is at a premium as well as everyone's inconvenience. My business is located on Charles St. which is a major north-south thoroughfare through the city and labeled as a snow emergency route. As such, there is no parking on the street itself. The nearest parking garage is four blocks away to the West. I mentioned this, because the only direct route from the garage to my office takes me in front of Ms. Rose's first floor apartment building directly across the street. The building itself is unique to the city because it can boast of its very rare front facing verandas. There, at least two people can sit outside and enjoy a meal or a morning cup of coffee while observing the comings and goings of city life. Ms. Rose, a gnarly looking old Greek woman, who one would affectionately refer to as the city's "conscience," or in the old days "a gossip," keeps me abreast of everything that is happening in the city. And, from all I can tell, lives on her veranda.

"Hey Jake, what's new?" is her usual morning greeting.

"Not much today Ms. Rose," I replied while ambulating onward.

"Did you find out who was sleeping with the banker's brother-in-law yet?" she inquired as I passed by where she was sitting.

"Even if I did Ms. Rose, you know I can't tell you, that's confidential," I replied crossing the street.

"You know I'm gonna' find out sooner or later," she said, raising her voice to my advancing back.

"I know that" I replied waving over my shoulder. "But I thought I would just postpone your surprise for a few more days, that's all." I smiled and she laughed simultaneously at this because we both knew we were right.

In my capacity as a private investigator, I've been involved in some interesting cases, noteworthy and memorable to troubling and heart wrenching.
Some, as simple as finding a lost pet, to those somewhat more involved regarding love, bank fraud, kidnapping, money laundering, etc. You name it,
I've seen it.
So, it didn't surprise me when I walked into the office and Doris told me that I'd received a letter, which was slid under my office door without postmarks or stamps. What was surprising was the texture of the envelope itself. Not your common variety of white stationery found at your local Office Depot, but a rich textured, almost velvety smooth cotton fabric. Slightly beige in color itself, it had been addressed with a calligraphy pen in a maroon ink by a discernably female hand. I was not a PI for nothing. And it had a distinct fragrance. One that could be hauntingly detected from afar and became almost intoxicating when held to the nose as I was doing at the moment. During my self-induced "timeout," I noticed that Doris was smirking in my direction.
"I didn't say anything," she said as she began faking some non-existing office work.

"Hmm" was all I replied as I walked into my inner sanctum; note in hand, smile on face, mind completely blank. It took me a couple of minutes to come out of my stupor, hang up my coat and pour myself a cup of coffee before I hit the chair behind my desk and began to scrutinize the note I held in my hand.

Just as I was preparing to open the letter, my intercom buzzed and Doris announced, "your brother is on line one. By the way, he stopped by the other day when you were out, and I told him I didn't know where you were or how long you would be away. He said that was 'OK', he would just 'hang out' in your office for a while and wait. I never did see him leave."

"Thanks," I told her.

With only a cursory glance at the letter I was holding, I picked up the phone.

"Hey bro, how's it hanging?" I said.

"As low as usual," he replied. Which was his typical response.

"What can I do you for?" I inquired.

"Are you busy?" he asked.

"For anybody else, yes. Not for you, what's up?"

"I think I'm in a little bit of trouble and I need your help," he replied.

This statement quickly diverted my attention away from the letter I was holding or any other thing I had on my mind because my brother, on the one hand, never got into trouble. And, on the other hand, seldom asked me for help. I was now quite concerned.

"You have my undivided attention," I said.

He went on to explain how he had just received notice from a music publisher claiming he was being sued for copyright infringement and plagiarism.

"How is this possible?" I inquired.

"I don't know exactly" he replied. "You remember that song that we wrote and recorded in '89? Well, I sent it off as a demo to a couple of record companies back then to see if it had potential as a "chart topper." But I never heard anything back from them. Somehow, it's now made its way onto several radio stations and this one music publisher heard it and is now suing me for the infractions that I told you about."

"That's ridiculous" I told him. "I was there when we both wrote it."

"I know, I don't get it" he said.

I asked him to give me the name and address of this 'music publisher' and told him not to worry. I'd look into the matter ASAP.

"Thanks a lot bro," he said. "I knew I could count on you."

"Hey, that's what brothers are for" I said.

After hanging up, I remembered back to that summer of '89. How we collaborated and struggled to get that song we had just jointly written as perfect as it could be. I know. I was there. And if my brother was guilty of what they were accusing him of, then so was I.

And that wasn't possible.

Chapter 6
A Plot Trist

After several minutes of staring bewilderingly into space while thinking of my brother, I noticed I was still holding the envelope. Curiosity getting the better of me, I opened it. Inside, written with the same delicate hand that had addressed the envelope was a note which read:

Mr. Rivers,

Both your experience and reputation as a private investigator have come to my attention in my time of need. My father, who I love dearly, has been missing for several days now, which is very unlike him, and I fear he has come to harm. I have not proved this myself so far and seek your help in this matter.
I'll be more than happy to compensate you for your time and trouble, no matter _what_ it costs. Enclosed is my telephone number. I will make myself available to you day or night.

Nina Thymins

Could the day get more bizarre?
First my brother, and now this Nina person. Strangely, I felt like I was being confused from both ends, morally from my brother and olfactorily from this unknown woman. (I could still smell the envelope I was holding). It was too late in the day to do anything about my brother's situation because it was past working hours, but I could make a phone call.

After three rings, a sultry voice answered the telephone. After verifying that the voice on the other end of the line was indeed thee Ms. Nina, the author of the letter, I told her my name. She thanked me for getting back to her so promptly and asked me if returning her call meant that I was going to accept her commission. Saying that the voice on the other end of the phone wasn't alluring was like claiming water wasn't wet. And there was a slight hint of an accent, whose origins I could not at the moment discern. If I didn't know better, I would swear I was talking to one of those 800 "phone for sex" calls you read about in the periodicals. I told her that her situation was intriguing but before I agreed to help her, I would need to have more information from her about the subject and that we would also need to meet in person. To this she agreed, and we formally arranged to meet the next day at two o'clock at Shane's, a little Bistro I frequented on Calvert St.

The next morning could not have gone any slower. The more I tried to will the hour hand to move faster, the more it seemed to resist my efforts. I made a telephone call to this so-called music publisher and arranged to meet with him the following morning at nine a.m. in his office located in downtown Philadelphia. I made a few more to my contacts in the industry as well. While initially doing my due diligence for my brother in researching the Phoenix Music Publishing Company Inc. and one of its producers, a mister Ian Hold, I could find no problems with their licensure, reputation, or past business dealings. So far.

At two o'clock that afternoon, I was perched in my usual window seat at Shane's, where I would, while having a cappuccino macchiato, enjoy the commotion of the city. In an odd way, I could empathize with Ms. Rose. Today however, I was eyeball deep into my laptop, caught up in the research I was doing for my brother, when the sound of the door opening to the café caught my attention, as did the woman who entered.
By her body language, you could immediately tell she was looking for someone. Petite in stature, she had auburn to black hair, cut short at the nape of her neck in a style similar to that worn by Meg Ryan during her heyday in the movies. I caught her eye, and she immediately began to walk towards me. And what a walk. To say it was attractive would be an understatement. Alluring would be more accurate. And in the back of my mind, I could hear Humphrey Bogart in Casablanca say, "of all the gin joints

In all the towns In all the world, she walks into mine."
Funny how your mind works. And I knew it was 'her'
before she even reached me because her envelopes
perfume preceded her. As we extended our hands in
introduction, all I could see of her was her eyes. Slightly
almond shaped and sapphire blue, they looked right into
you. Not "at" you as is the case when most people look at
each other, but straight into your soul. Well, that is the
way it felt to me anyhow. And in doing so, in their
reflection, I could see the faces of my children. I knew
right then and there that I was in deep shit.

At that same moment, in a high-rise building in
downtown Philadelphia, an elderly gentleman sitting
behind a desk at the Phoenix Music Publishing Company
was talking to several of his associates in a thick Russian
accent.
"They are meeting as we speak. When he is here
tomorrow, I want him led down the well of his brothers'
problems so deep that he doesn't have time for anything
else. Is that understood?" From his obvious demeanor and
delivery, it was almost impossible not to understand his
meaning.
His associates, who could be described as nothing less
than thugs from right out of the Al Capone era, in
acquiescence to his demand, said not a word but lowered
both their eyes and their heads in unison.

Chapter 7
The Commission

As I pulled up a second chair and invited her to sit down,
she glanced nervously around the café. I didn't place too
much stock in the gesture, then.

"Tell me a little bit about your father" I asked.

"What does he do for a living?"

"He's in the textile import and export business,"
she replied.

"And what specific textiles does he import and export?" I
asked.

She said she wasn't exactly sure. I found that response to
be interesting and slightly suspicious due to the way she
averted her eyes when she spoke. But I let it slide for now.

"When and where was the last time you saw him?"
I inquired.

"About two weeks ago in Moscow," she answered.

I've been through Moscow during one of my work-related
travels out West. Quaint little "Arts" town on the
Washington border. It can brag about being the home of
the University of Idaho but not much more. I did not
recall it being the hub of an industrial textile import and
export business the last time I was through there and I
told her as much. At this statement, she trained those
sapphire eyes right through mine while developing the
cutest smirk at the corner of her mouth.

"Russia," was all she said.

"Russia? You mean Russia as in Russia?" I asked dumbfoundedly while stretching my arm towards the window as far as it would extend. As though Rand McNally's world map was hanging just off the end of my finger.

"As in Mother Russia" she replied broadening her smile. This statement in and of itself gave me pause. But now the accent made sense. I asked her to please elaborate.

She went on to explain that as an arts professor at the M.V. Lomonosov State University, her class schedule was such that she had Tuesday afternoons off, and she usually met her father for lunch at their favorite local restaurant. Two weeks ago, he never showed up and she has not seen or heard from him since then. She had been raised by her father after her mother passed away when she was young, and they have always been very close. He would never have left voluntarily without leaving her word of where he was going and how long he would be away.

The same scenario was true as reported from his work associates and close friends.

I asked her if she had shared her concern with the local authorities. At this statement, her face grew solemn, and her voice determined. She explained to me that unless you wanted the Russian police, or worse, to start looking into your private lives, you didn't bring up matters such as this to them unless it was completely unavoidable. Or, of extreme national interest.

This statement I acknowledged with an affirmative head shake.

"And what brings you to this side of the pond?" I inquired. At this statement, her face wrinkled slightly as in deep thought as her eyes darted around the floor to see, as if by some miracle, a pond had mysteriously appeared in the forest of cafe chairs to explain which side of it she was sitting on. Internally enjoying her confusion for a few seconds, I went on to explain what the statement meant as far as our brothers in England were concerned. Looking nonplussed by this strange explanation, she went on to tell me that she had the opportunity to teach a class here at the University of Maryland on a topic in her field of study and while here, she decided to seek professional help in her quest to find her father. She said she began inquiring into finding local investigators when colleagues of hers, here at the university, brought my name to her attention. Also, the fact that I had helped a friend of theirs, a Ms. Smith, some years ago locate her missing daughter. I do recall helping a woman by that name, but I didn't realize I had made such an impression. The dots were coming together. Not all of them, but enough to satiate my curiosity for now. Not regarding motive or causation but need. It was in acknowledging her need for help that I agreed to help her. In response to revealing my decision to her, she slowly leaned toward me across the table, and with her eyes growing moist, reached out and gently clasped my hands.

"Thank you" was all she said.

Did I mention to you how deep in shit I knew I was? I could have stayed in this poignant tableau all day, but she broke my reverie by announcing that if she didn't leave quite soon, she was going to be late for one of her classes. We agreed to resume this conversation in greater detail at our next meeting. We scheduled one for late tomorrow afternoon in my office. I never believed in the old fairy tale adage, "love at first sight." Not until now, that is. As she sauntered her way to the exit, 'Serpentine style' through the cafe chairs, I didn't know whether I had just made the worst mistake of my life, or if I had just made the best mistake of my life. Presently, all I could think of was, "Road Trip!"

Chapter 8
Going down the record hole

I already mentioned that I wasn't a morning person. I like to give my mind and my body adequate time in which to come to an equal state of readiness. Anything could throw off this delicate balance. Drinking excessively in the evening or having a late date or both could throw off crucial decision making the next morning. Similarly, participating in my favorite charities 5K race could potentially interfere with my body's ability to successfully run down a fleeing fugitive that evening. Everything in moderation and everything in its own time. You may quote me. But for the life of me, I could not get Mr. Hold's secretary to give me an appointment later than nine o'clock in the morning.

"Scheduling conflicts" she admitted.

Although the hour was inhuman, the trip to Philadelphia wasn't too bad. It's basically a straight shot up I-95. Getting into Philadelphia, however, is a pain in the butt. It's only saving grace is that it's not Washington DC. Commuting in Washington tops my list. It took me just as long to get through Philadelphia as it did to get to Philadelphia. At the peak of rush hour traffic, it was just gridlock to gridlock. Anticipating this dilemma, however, I left early enough to be at the Phoenix Music Publishing Company a good fifteen minutes ahead of my appointment time. This "time perk" was quickly obliterated, by the fact that Mr. Holds' secretary had me cooling my heels in the waiting room a good half an hour past my appointment time. In the interim, putting my investigative mind to work, because I hate wasting time, I decided to check out the Décor. The building in general was furnished in early period, "We've got more money than we know what to do with" to modern, "And you'll never be as important as us."

When I finally did get the call to go to see him, one could say my mood was not as pleasant as when I had arrived. And it was going downhill from there. Entering his office, I was greeted, and I use the term loosely, not by one man as expected, but by two. Neither one of them introduced themselves by name when I did and declined to shake hands. One was short and overweight, and resembled Telly Savalas from the TV show Kojak. The other one drew a remarkable resemblance to Lurch of Addams Family fame. 'Lurch' never said a word. 'Kojack' did all the talking. And when he spoke, he sounded just like Nina. Russian? Odd. He informed me that they were associates of Mr. Holds and handed me an envelope that they claimed contained all the pertinent information I needed to know about my brothers' infractions and their legal standing in the business. The one thing that 'pisses me off' when doing business, is that if I make time to meet with the concerned party, you know, 'Party of the first part'. They should make time to meet with me; 'Party of the second part'. I don't like negotiating with anybody's lackeys. Especially these two. Their very demeanor made you suspicious of

them personally and anything they had to say to you. And, they resembled casting rejects from an Untouchables film. I couldn't glean any more pertinent information about my brother's dilemma from them verbally, for they just deferred to the envelope they had just given me. After a few more minutes of what I perceived was one sided banter, I decided staying any longer would be unproductive and not worth my time or effort. As I prepared to leave, 'Kojak' informed me, in a 'not-so-subtle' inference, that Mr. Hold would not be getting back to me in the future "directly."
Any further inquiries I was to make about this case was to be managed through his secretary.
"You may leave by way of the door you came in," he announced as a formal way of dismissal. Good thing I play a mean game of poker, because if it wasn't for the control I have over my facial musculature, the obvious 'tell' that I would have forecast of "eat shit and die" would have been blatantly apparent. And that was the nicer expression of the few dozen I was contemplating.

On the drive home, I kept hoping that indeed all the information I needed to know about my brother's case was in the envelope sitting on the front passenger seat. Because contemplating going back up to where I just left, made me both angry and nauseous, simultaneously. The only thing that was brightening my very dismal mood, was the thought of meeting Nina this afternoon in my office.

Chapter 9

"Second verse, same as the first"

When I got to the office, Doris knew something was amiss from the way I was acting. You can't hide anything from Doris. I informed her that I was meeting a new client this afternoon, and that she was to clear the rest of my docket, as well as cancel the calls that I was to make or return for the rest of the day. She looked at me askance as if saying "what are you up to?" I kept pacing around the inside of my office, like a caged animal, while glancing at the unopened envelope containing my brother's information I had placed on top of my desk when I arrived. I knew I should be getting to this as soon as possible, but I didn't want to start something and then have to stop in the middle when Nina arrived. I promised myself that when I got home later today, I would attack it with both feet, 'long jump' style.

As if the mere thought of her could make her magically appear, I looked through my office door and out the front window and saw her across the street, in person. As I made my way to the front door and she made her way across the street, I couldn't help but recognize my own heightened anticipation of our second meeting. I opened the door to her now familiar smile and gentle "hello." As she walked past me entering the office, I also noticed the

same enticing perfume I had been entranced by
previously. As I preceded to close the door, breaking my
brief reverie, I could have sworn I saw the 'Kojak and
Lurch' clones turn the corner a block away driving a black
sedan. Our meeting this morning must have upset me
more than I thought. Pushing that encounter quickly to
the back of my mind, for I had better things to currently
occupy my thoughts, I closed the door. I introduced the
two young ladies, who amicably shook hands and greeted
each other warmly, then directed Nina by way of gesture
to my private office. Allowing the lady to precede me
through the doorway, as all gentlemen should, garnered
me a few seconds to look back in Doris's direction. She
elevated both eyebrows in an "Oh yeah?" expression,
which was returned promptly by my own Groucho Marx's
eyebrow "hubba-hubba" response.

As I turned around to continue entering my office, I
realized I wasn't following Nina any longer. As a matter of
fact, she was nowhere to be seen and I was quite alone. As
my eyes rapidly scanned the room, my brain was trying to
rationalize this irrational scenario. I slowly tiptoed into the
room while further opening the door, calling her name in
a whispered sing-song voice as a parent would to a child
playing hide and seek. "Nina?.......Neenah?"
As I reached the apex of the doors opening, I realized my
ears were picking up sounds of very shallow, rapid, and
irregular intakes of air coming from behind the door. As I
glanced around the door's edge, there she was.
Slightly pale and trembling. Her back plastered against
the wall and trying to disappear in the door's shadow.

"Neenah?" I whisper-called once more coming a little closer. What an idiot, I said in self-chastisement. In my zealousness to get Nina back to my inner office, I completely forgot to forewarn her about Babe. Usually, I would broach this subject with clients in the outer office over a cup of coffee while talking to Doris. In Nina's case, I completely forgot.

Her lovely eyes had fixated on a point in space somewhere farther into the room. She raised an unsteady index finger. Keeping it purposefully as close to her chest as she could while pointing, in an almost inaudible voice, through trembling lips whispered, " s..s..s..sNAKE!!" While Babe, some three feet away in her enclosed glass aquarium, was similarly regarding her new playmate, Nina, with the same intense stare. I, on the other hand, was not paying the least bit of attention to the scene that was developing right in front of me. As soon as Nina spoke, my subconscious mind fixated on her lips. And from the dream I had the other night, my subconscious mind wanted to do more to her lips at this moment than watch them tremble. The thought of "trembling lips" brought my consciousness back to the present, instantaneously.

"Nina, it's OK," I said in my best motherly voice. "She's a pet and perfectly harmless." Upon my uttering this statement, Nina's head and eyes slowly rotated in order to look at me, and with an outward facial expression of "YOU'VE GOT TO BE KIDDING," her lips pantomimed, "A PET?"

"Yes, a pet. She was a present from a former client and a story for another day." "Come," I said, "let me introduce you." While saying this, I simultaneously reached out and touched her left, non-pointing hand. She immediately wrapped her whole body around my right arm; like a piece of cellophane would envelope a left-over Thanksgiving drumstick. Or a child her father's leg while playing "merry-go-round" in the house. Her gesture brought out in me a protective empathy and the largest smile I didn't think I was capable of making.
"It's H..U..G..E," she stammered. My smile, if at all possible, got bigger.
While still locked in her "death grip," Nina and I proceeded, in tandem, to shuffle toward the aquarium. As we got closer to the glass enclosure, Babe's stare and Nina's grip intensified.
"Nina, this is Babe. Babe, this is Nina." At the sound of her own name, Babe's hood expanded to all its magnificence.
And Nina fainted.

Chapter 10
Once more, with Feeling

"I think she's coming around," Doris declared while exchanging one wet compress for a colder one. While groaning softly, Nina's eyelids fluttered open. She found herself lying, quite comfortably, supine on the couch in my inner office with Doris at her head and me, kneeling alongside, patting her hands.

"I'm so sorry," I said apologetically, "I should have warned you."

"That's OK," she said sitting up slowly, "I'm usually not taken by surprise, and I've never been prone to fainting, but" … and she let the rest of the sentence hang while groaning and feeling her forehead.

"Listen," I said, "we can do this some other time when you're feeling a little better."

"No, no!" she insisted, "I wanted to spend more time with you to . . to . . to go over the situation concerning my father," she stammered. At this comment, Doris and I exchanged a knowing glance.

"OK" I said, "but we'll have to do it in here." Following this statement, she began to grow pale again. I explained, "All my audio and video recording devices are in this room, and I like to have a permanent record of all my interviews. Tell you what I'll do. I'll go get Babe's night hood and cover her entire tank so you can't see her. She'll fall asleep and you won't hear a peep out of her for

the rest of the day."
Upon hearing this, Nina looked skeptical, to say the least.
"Promise" I said, holding my open palm up facing her, as
one does during a court trial and the swearing in process.
"Promise?" she implored.
"Promise" I said, crossing my heart and twisting my
fingers. This got a little giggle and a smile at of her, and I
knew we were in business.

Chapter 11
"The facts ma'am, just the facts"

After the meeting that afternoon in my office with Nina, I went home to pour over the material in the manila envelope regarding my brother and his lawsuit. Nina left the office saying that she had to prepare for her lectures that were taking place at the University of Maryland in College Park all the next morning. As productive as our meeting was, her apparent eager departure was, 'understandable.'

During our session, Nina told me that her father's name was Yuri Petroff and that he was an auditor in the accounting department of the Bryansk Worsted Company of textile importers and exporters in Russia.

"Petroff?" I asked inquisitively. Noting my confused expression she said,

"I took the last name of my mother to honor her memory."

I acknowledge this admission with the nod of my head. She went on to say that while auditing the company's books, her father found monetary and descriptive discrepancies between its inventory, sales and purchasing facts pertaining to the last few years. He suspected fraud from within the company and brought his concern to the attention of his superiors. Two weeks later, he disappeared. I remarked that we couldn't make too much more headway with this case while here in the United States and we would have to make plans on going to

Russia to continue the investigation. She acknowledged the wisdom in this strategy and said that she would start making travel plans for us tomorrow. She said the timing couldn't be better because she was wrapping up her lecture series at the end of next week and was planning to go home thereafter anyway. She said that she would take the next week as well, to write down any pertinent information i.e., names, addresses and telephone numbers that she knew about her father and his colleagues for my research, prior to our arrival in Russia. I told her that would be extremely helpful, and we left it at that.

Before I left the office, I stopped by to see Doris and asked her to look up any information she could find about a Yuri Petroff and the Bryansk Worsted Company out of Russia; to let Babe out of her enclosure and to let the banker's wife know that I would be calling her in the morning with an update.

"I'm going home to do some research for my brother and tomorrow morning I'll be in Washington."

"More research?" she asked.

"What else," I said.

In the stack of papers that were given to me by the Phoenix Publishing Company lackeys, there were dozens of individual and company names of those suing my brother for copyright infringements. The first thing I did was to research those names to verify their authenticity. In doing so, I started down, what would become over the next several days, the long road of confusion. I found and verified the names of several individuals as well as companies themselves, but could not connect them, individually or collectively to each other, any recording, publishing, or legal agencies or to my brother specifically. If this was Phoenix's big case against my brother, I wasn't impressed, so far. I could only do so much investigating from my home computer and decided to devote more of my energies at the source, and that would be tomorrow in Washington.

At the 'crack of dawn,' my witching hour, with coffee in hand, I was in my car and heading south down I-95. I was looking forward to driving through Washington about as much as I would have enjoyed shooting myself in the foot. And I can tell you from past experience, the latter is not pleasant at all. And NO, I did not shoot myself in the foot. That 'honor' was given to me by another. In the line of duty and such. My destination this morning was the Library of Congress and their copyright division.

The Library of Congress is the largest library in the world, with millions of books, films and videos, audio recordings, photographs, newspapers, maps and manuscripts in its collections. The Library of Congress occupies three buildings on Capitol Hill. The Thomas Jefferson building, the John Adams building, and the James Madison memorial building. Other facilities include the high-density storage facility at Fort Meade Maryland, and the Packard campus for audio visual conservation in Culpeper, Virginia. Today, I was headed for the James Madison memorial building at 101 Independence Ave, SE Washington.

When an artist creates a piece of intellectual property, as my brother and I did in the summer of '89 by writing a song for instance, it is automatically copyrighted. By the sheer fact of setting down on paper or audio tape or in some instances canvas, modeling clay or film; as soon as the idea becomes reality, it is copyrighted. It is a good idea, however, in order to protect this piece of intellectual property from those who wish to steal it and profit from it in any way in the future, i.e., to have the fact that you created it "first" documented.

That is exactly what my brother and I did that summer. We transcribed the music to paper as well as audio tape and sent both to the Library of Congress. There, a sophisticated team of professionals as well as supercomputers looked over not only the notes and the melody and the combination of all the above but the lyrics and their association to the music as well. There, the patterns were scrutinized and deemed "unique," that is, uncommon to any other similar entity that preceded it. Thus, it was deemed an original, and granted an official copyright.

There are different copyright laws governing the right of songs versus that of just music or just poetry because a song is a combination of both. And as such, is governed by different copyright laws. And the laws in and of themselves are not infinite. All works published in the United States before 1924 are in the public domain, meaning anyone may use them/it without penalty or restriction. Works published after 1923, but before 1978

are protected for 95 years from the date of publication. If the work was created, but not published, before 1978, the copyright lasts for the life of the author plus 70 years. Having created this particular entity in 1989, my brother's protection under said laws is ensured. And we have the library of congresses ID catalog numbers to prove it. Today, in the era of the Internet, one can simply upload a tune to YouTube for instance, and within several minutes, the supercomputers of the web could tell you if what you just whistled into the phone is original.
We didn't have that luxury in '89.

In general, copyright laws have two purposes. The first is to provide continuing incentives encouraging people to develop creative works. The second is to facilitate productive use of creative content by the public. Sometimes these two purposes conflict with each other. A perfect example of this would be the current situation regarding the singing of a particularly 'well know' song, I'm sure you've noticed. Certain restaurants that, in the past, used to celebrate your birthday by singing the traditional "Happy Birthday" song at your table while presenting you with a dessert of their choice in gratitude for your patronage, have ceased doing so. Strange rhythmic clapping or unfamiliar chants have now replaced it. That's because, contrary to what you have heard about Michael Jackson or Paul McCartney's ownership of same, the publishing rights to "happy birthday to you" is owned by the Warner Music company. The company itself doesn't care if you walk outside and

sing the song to the tree in your backyard, because they're
not making any royalties from it. If people who work in
restaurants however, and getting paid to be there, are
performing duties assigned to them by the restaurant
itself, which, in this case, include the singing of a song
that's contributing to their making a profit,
Warner Brothers wants its "cut."
"Follow the money" I always say, "follow the money."
And that is exactly what I was presently doing.

Performing hours of research in the stacks of the largest
library in the world was not my idea of having fun. And
the long road of confusion was getting even longer. From
all I could tell, no one person or company or entity was, or
is filing a claim against my brother, myself or the
copyright laws protecting his intellectual property. I didn't
know what game Ian Hold was playing, and by this
'inning,' I assure you, I didn't like his rules, but I was
coming home to find out. But first and foremost,
I needed to talk to my brother.

Chapter 12
Hello, anybody home?

I like surprises, don't you? I like them so much that I like to share them. And at this point in my day, I couldn't think of a better person to share a surprise with than Nina. And wouldn't you know it, she was just up the street. The University of Maryland, located on the College Park campus, my old alma mater, was just a stone's throw off of Rt. 50. The exact road on which I was currently driving. How convenient. Taking "Campus drive" to the heart of the university, I set my sights on the administration offices. Entering the building through the white column facade brought back fond memories like a welcome friend.

"I'm looking for a professor, here from Russia, who's giving a lecture on art history this morning. Her name is Nina Thymins. Do you know where I could find her?" I inquired to the woman behind the desk.

"Just a minute, let me check" she said as she began typing multiple commands into her computer. As she began her research, I couldn't help but mentally reminisce about the years I spent on this campus. Both in the classrooms, in the beer halls and at the frat houses and the combination of all the above. Not to mention my brief, but meaningful relationship with their track and field organization as a pole vaulter. From a scholastic point of view, I wondered where I found time to do any socializing. From a 'drinking' point of view, I wondered how I learned anything whatsoever.

"I can't find anyone by that name associated with the university" she said in a bewildered voice.

"Let me check the schedules."

"That's odd, I don't have any art history lectures scheduled for today or even this week" she exclaimed.

That long road I mentioned was now turning into a highway.

"Are you sure?" I asked. "Nina Thymins. From Russia. Art history teacher."

"No, nothing at all" she answered. "And one other thing" she said while looking confused.

"The university hasn't utilized their foreign lecture series grants in the last six months. No one from overseas has given any lectures here since then."

After thanking her for her efforts, and making my way back to my car, I just sat there, perplexed. In front of me was the lawn that ran up to the Chapel. Everyone called it a 'lawn,' but it was bigger than two football fields. And if we weren't playing flag football on it, we were protesting the war from its 'fescued' surface. In front of that lay "fraternity row." A horseshoe shaped driveway enclosing its own football sized athletic field. Around its outer perimeter rose a dozen of what would have been called in the South, 'Tara-esque' mansions, supposedly occupied by the best and brightest of the campus's student academia.

Not to mention, hosting the greatest parties you could possibly imagine during the school year. Just beyond that, and out of sight from where I was sitting, but not out of

range of my olfactory senses, was the Department of
Agriculture.
If my academic years here taught me anything, it was to
think for myself. Process and disseminate information.
The information I had been accumulating all week wasn't
adding up, 'et al', and trying to disseminate it was giving
me a headache. The solution to this dilemma, I
rationalized, was the need to acquire more information.
Ergo,
there were a lot of people I needed to talk to this
afternoon, and I wasn't accomplishing that
just sitting here.

Chapter 13
Peekaboo

Being "lost in thought " is an expression everyone has heard of and experienced sometime in their lives. And it doesn't usually surprise them when they find themselves "in the zone." It did surprise me, however, when I realized I was standing in front of Ms. Rose's veranda and had no idea how I got there. And, for that matter, what I was doing in the city. Obviously, I deduced, I was going to my office.

"Lost Jake?" exclaimed Ms. Rose.

"What?" I said spontaneously, not realizing who had just called my name.

"Never mind," she said in her grumpy demeanor while ignoring my bewilderment.

"I see business is picking up," she queried.

"I don't know what you mean," I answered still confused. "I'm assuming with all the recent comings and goings that business is picking up. The young woman who came and left your office this morning and now the two 'business looking' gentlemen who just went in a few minutes ago" she stated.

Mentally scratching my head, because I didn't have a meeting scheduled with Nina today, I admitted to myself unbiasedly. And nothing or no one was scheduled for this afternoon whatsoever. It wasn't until my mind focused on the latter part of her statement regarding the "two gentlemen" that my consciousness crystallized. It was neither uncommon nor unusual to entertain male clients in my office, but not as a 'tag team.' The only Duo that I could think of was . . .

"Business couldn't be better" I declared to Ms. Rose as a farewell statement while striding determinately across the street.

Pausing at the corner of my building, my internal detective asked me, "why are they here and what do they want?"

I wasn't about to go through the front door to find out. So, I detoured down the alley on the side of my building toward the back door. Plan B. I hesitated again when realizing that the rear door had an alarm system that would alert anyone in the office that it had been opened. Looking around for a solution, I spied the fire escape which led to the roof. Plan C.

While climbing the ladder, I came to the realization that its deteriorated, and deteriorating condition was going to lead to someone's imminent demise while trying to escape their imminent demise. And I hoped it would not be me. After barely making it safely to the roof, I stealthy made my way over to the skylight. The skylight itself not only let sunlight illuminate my outer office but allowed an unobstructed view directly onto Doris's desk. There, not to my surprise, sat Doris surrounded by 'Heckle and Jeckle.' I didn't like them the first time I met them, and I wasn't liking them anymore today. They had taken up menacing positions while corralling Doris to her desk. The short, heavy-set, "Telly Savalas" looking gent, had his right buttocks parked on the right corner of her desk next to the telephone. The tall, "Lurch" looking personage, was positioned directly behind her and to her left. It wasn't difficult to conclude that Doris was being harassed. It was also obvious that they were waiting for me. My dislike for them began to increase. It was during moments such as this that I began to earn my paycheck.

Realizing there was no reason for them to stay if I wasn't coming in, I put my plan into operation. I pulled my cell phone out of my pocket and dialed the office phone knowing that Doris always had the speaker phone enabled. The office phone began to ring two floors below my lofty position on the roof. My suspicions of 'the Duos' ill intent were confirmed when I saw the 'Telly Savalas' clone gesture to Doris to answer the phone and leave the speaker option on.

"Mr. Rivers office," Doris stated with her usual professional intonation.

"Hey Doris, it's me. Do me a favor and reschedule my three o'clock appointment today with Miss Hillbinger for tomorrow at five." Lying, and knowing that I was lying, she replied, "sure Jake, anything else I can do for you?"

"Yeah" I said, "I'm not coming in for the rest of the day, so be a dear and lock up the office when you leave."

"Can do," she answered.

"Thanks" I said and hung up. In hoping my admission produced the desired result, I maneuvered my way, as quickly as I dared, down the fire escape to the alley. From there, I made my way back up to the street but stayed purposefully inside the alley's shadow. It wasn't long after I heard the outer office door close that the foremost of the two hoodlums entered the alley entrance where I was waiting.

"Looking for me?" I said in a loud, declaratory voice. Anticipating the startled reaction of my nearest guest, I ducked just in time to avoid his left cross to my right temple while simultaneously connecting an uppercut of my own directly into his solar plexus. The audible expulsion of bronchial air was followed swiftly by the collapse to his knees. Unfortunately for me, the collapse of hoodlum number one blocked my egress to his partner's position, which allowed him to evade my pursuit and make a timely escape. Having to be satisfied with my single conquest, I slapped him in the handcuffs I conveniently store on my belt and dragged his ass into my office through the back door.

"Good Work Doris!" I shouted while observing her crossed armed posture, smirking face, and ramrod straight back as she stood by her desk.

"s'bout time," she answered as she walked over and opened the bathroom door. The bathroom has become our preferred holding cell to date when we host vermin such as our present company. Doris had to help me drag his sorry carcass into the bathroom, because he was becoming uncooperative. I took the end of the handcuff that wasn't on his wrist and clamped it tight to the radiator. While he was attempting to acclimate to his lowly position on the floor, I couldn't help but comment that "it might not be the Hilton, but you have to admit, you can't beat the price."

"Now," I said, making myself comfortable sitting on the toilet lid, "what are you doing here?" To this question, there was no reply from our guest. Not completely unexpected.

"Let me guess. Asking any more straightforward questions is going to get me the same reply?"

Again, only silence.

"OK, have it your way" I said standing up.

"Stay there and behave yourself," I said to no one in particular as I slammed the door while walking back into the office.

In answer to Doris's wide-eyed expression, I held my index finger to my lips and said as loud as possible for anyone in the next building to have heard, "he gets bread and water once a day until I get what I want to know."

She stifled a giggle as we turned the lights off, set the buildings alarms and departed. 'Time will tell' they say, and because I was dead serious, I was willing to wait.

While crossing the street, Doris and I parted company because she was parked in the opposite direction of my parking garage. If I were as intuitive as I believed myself to be, I wouldn't have gotten caught in Ms. Roses 'laser stare' as I approached her veranda. But it did prepare me for her third degree.

"Knocking off a little early today huh Jake?" she inquired. "Business that good?"

"Different day, same dollar" I replied as I made my way
past her sentry post.
"Ain't that the truth," she chuckled.

While walking to my car, I tried calling Nina as well as my
brother and got no answer from either. I decided my
brother was number one on my agenda, so I headed over
to the studio to see if I could catch him at work.

Chapter 14
"Bro, what the F...?"

I made my way over to my brother's studio by the shortest possible route I knew. As I was pulling into the parking lot out back, I noticed a familiar sedan pulling out of the parking lot out front. And wouldn't you know it, 'Abbott,' of the "Abbott and Costello" henchman was driving. So now, they were putting on the full court "harassment" press, I thought to myself. I knew my brother was here because his car was parked in its usual parking spot. I entered the studio as usual through the back door.

"Hey!" I shouted coming into the room. At this my brother almost jumped out of his shoes.

"Oh, it's you," he said in obvious relief.

"I see you had some company?" I inquired gesturing with my thumb towards the back door.

"What do you mean?" he asked, looking confused.

"The 'Lurch clone' from the publishing company that I just saw leave" I stated with my hands going to my hips. This statement seemed to confuse my brother even more because he just stood there and stared at me.

"The guy that just left; the same guy with his ugly twin that I met at the publishing company the other day; the ones that are suing you for copyright infringements, those guys" I shouted.

"Oh yeah, yeah.... those guys," he said coming out of his momentary stupor.

"Listen," I began, "if they're harassing you, just tell me and I'll take care of it. I already caught one harassing Doris this morning and I got his ass locked up, handcuffed in my bathroom. I've been doing my homework, and I'm gonna' tell you right now, while looking into all the legal ramifications of this lawsuit, I don't see much to it."
After this pronouncement, my brother's stupor seemed to return as he comatosely walked over to me, patted me on the shoulder, and thanked me for all the efforts I was making on his behalf. He then nonchalantly claimed he had some business that was urgent he needed to take care of, and without further ado or goodbye, exited through the back door.
I stood there for a few moments pondering what had just happened. Because I was the only one there in the room and didn't see any immediate resolution to the multiple questions I just mentally asked myself, I decided to leave.
On the way out to the car I decided to call Nina. I was hoping to get more answers to my questions concerning her, than I did out of my brother just a moment ago.
There was still no answer.
On that note, and I mentally congratulated myself on the appropriate reference I just made, secondary to leaving 'a music' studio, I decided to go home. Might as well get a good night's sleep, because that road to confusion was getting wider and longer, and longer and wider.....

Chapter 15
"Cat got your tongue?"

After a day of bread and water, our bathroom guest was no more cooperative than the first day he arrived. Both I and my staff were becoming increasingly annoyed at both his silence and his presence. Opening the bathroom door, I noticed that there was a great deal more ecchymosis around his wrists, as well as traces of blood on the handcuffs themselves and the floor surrounding the radiator. I couldn't give two hoots about his disheveled appearance, but he was beginning to smell. I took my usual perch on the toilet seat, and in my most judicial manner asked, "Well?"

His answer to this was his usual silent staring contest with the wall.

I stood up disgustedly and began to leave the room saying to the atmosphere itself, "OK, I've had enough of this," and departed to my inner sanctum. When I returned carrying a large basket, our guest gave me an inquisitive but nasty glare. I placed the basket in the bathtub next to the radiator where our guest was handcuffed, lifted the lid, and said aloud, "now you two play nice together" and preceded to depart. At the threshold, I turned back just in time to see Babe's head rise above the confines of her basket. She was singing in her lovely Serpentine "hiss" while displaying all the plumage that only a cobra can deliver. As she locked eyes on her new captive playmate, she rose several more inches above the tub ledge. Upon seeing this vision materialize right in front of him, our guest became quite rigid. The look on his face went from agitated to starstruck and his eyes got bigger than basketballs. I couldn't help but chuckle as I closed the door. I didn't have long to wait so I can't say that the anticipation was killing me. After a minute of utter silence, followed by a minute of high-pitched screaming, I got all the information that I needed.

I subsequently unchained him from the radiator. Doris and I then dragged him down the steps to the basement where I re-handcuffed him to the water pipes. I was beginning to like this part of the investigation. I moved him, being the considerate host that I was, downstairs to the basement, because it would be nice and quiet and a change of scenery for him. I needed to get him out of the bathroom anyhow, because he was interfering with my other clients. And nobody could use the bathroom with him in there.

Back upstairs, before I entered my office, Doris handed me an envelope.

"Concerning Mr. Petroff," she stated. I took the envelope and walked into my office, closing the door behind me.

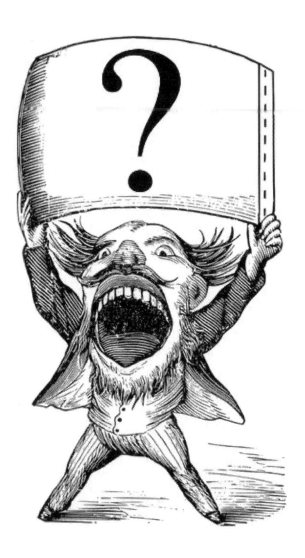

Chapter 16
What's my line?

After reading the information contained in the envelope, I immediately picked up the telephone and called Nina. She answered this time, and I told her, with emphatic determination, that I needed to meet with her immediately in my office.

"What's so urgent?" she asked.

"I'll tell you when you get here," I said and promptly hung up.

I wasn't waiting for her by the front door this time when she came to the office. She passed by Doris's desk, receiving a not so friendly look, as Doris picked up the office intercom and announced,

"Miss Thymins' here."

To which I replied, "send her in."

Doris only nodded toward her as a gestural sign of "go right in." I didn't bother covering the aquarium. This 'fact' was readily apparent to Nina as soon as she opened the door. She made her way sheepishly over to the chair adjacent to mine and sat down. With an "I don't know what you want to talk to me about, but you don't look happy to see me" expression on her face, I said to her, "guess where I went yesterday?" She delicately shook her head and shrugged her shoulders in an apparent, "I don't know" response.

"I went to see my favorite client. And do you know where that was?" I asked.

Again, that same response.

"I drove to the University of Maryland at College Park to see my favorite Russian art teacher conduct a class in art history. And do you know what?" She was beginning to look grave. A definite negative 'tell.'

"She wasn't there" I declared with a slight emphatic inflection. At this point, her tears were flowing quite freely from those almond shaped eyes.

As she lifted her hands to cover her face, I continued.

"And I also discovered some interesting details about a 'Yuri Petroff'. There doesn't seem to be much concerning him and his employer, Bryansk Worsted. In fact, they had never heard of him. But there is, or should I say, was a Yuri Petroff working for the Ministry of The Interior and the Museum of Natural History as a Geologist!

Care to explain? And the truth would be refreshing," said I.

"I'm sorry" she cried. "I thought if I told you the truth, you wouldn't have believed me. And I need you to believe me because I need your help."

She continued to sob into her hands as Babe reared her head at the sound and hissed at me from her enclosure as if to say, "now look what you did, you made her cry."

Two against one. Boy, I hate those odds. And when I looked through my office door window; make that three against one.

"OK" I said, handing her my handkerchief. "You've got my undivided attention. I'm all yours." And deep down, I really meant it.

She began by saying that her name really was Nina Thymins and her father's name is Yuri Petroff. And I was right, in that he worked for the Department of the Interior and was on the board of the Museum of Natural History. He also was a consultant to the **De Beers Consolidated Mining Company** out of South Africa as well as senior consultant to **Sotheby's at their Hong Kong location she added**. At this point, I was sitting straighter in my chair. She once again confirmed that her name was indeed Nina Thymins, and that she also worked for the Department of the Interior and the Museum of Natural History but not as an art director, as a Diamantaire. When my look told her I wasn't quite sure of what that meant, she went on to explain that she was an expert in the study of, and appraisal of diamonds. That got my curiosity. She continued by saying that she did use her mother's last name out of respect, originally 'Thyminskya', but changed it to 'Thymins' secondary to the insistence of her father as she began her advanced studies. Seeing that the two of them were in the same related field, her father didn't want any conflicts of interest or appearances of favoritism by those in the industry and scientific community in which they worked. And, as it turned out, most people didn't know they were related.

Months ago, while working for **De Beers** on location in South Africa, her father was instrumental in the discovery of a very large diamond. And by large, she meant earth and industry shattering.

He brought it back to Russia, and to her, where it was her job to appraise the diamond for both De Beers and Sotheby and the world for that matter. Her father had intended, through his connections with the government, as well as historical societies, that the government would eventually procure the diamond and display it as a national treasure. She went on to claim that Russia is the largest collector and owner of diamonds in the world. A fact of which I was not aware. Until now. This diamond, now affectionately known as "Nothing" by those in the industry, and she went on to explain why, was probably the largest documented diamond to date in the world.

"A week ago, the diamond came up for sale" she explained. "That is, it came up for auction at Sotheby. I was there, and so was your brother."

"WHAT?" I shouted nearly coming out of my chair. "My brother?"

"Yes," she said, "let me continue." As a member of the Industry, the Museum, and the appraiser of the diamond, she explained to me she had a right to be there. As a matter of fact, she had a duty to uphold. That was, to inspect the diamond and its corresponding paperwork one last time before the auction.

"When I went down to the vault," she stated, "I saw men there who should not have been there. They didn't see me, but I recognized them." She paused here, gathering her thoughts.

"Well, who were...?"

"Please" she said, "let me continue." "I waited for them to leave and then went in to do my due diligence. The diamond appeared to be fine, but the paperwork accompanying it was wrong. As a matter of fact, it wasn't my appraisal at all. It had the correct name of the diamond printed on the invoice, but both the 4C's and GIA graded values were wrong. Seriously wrong. And much lower than they should have been. I left to inform someone about my discovery when the auction started. I didn't know what to do at that moment, so I just watched. The auctioneer announced the correct name of the diamond, but gave the incorrect values for its description, aloud, resulting in uncharacteristic and bizarre bidding, and, in the end, the diamond sold for much less than it's worth. I didn't understand it then, but I do now. I told you my father disappeared two weeks ago. He did not. He was murdered. And I saw who did it. It was the same men that I saw down at the vault that day. It's the mob. The 'Bratva.' The Russian mafia. They changed the official documentation concerning the diamond and created a forgery. Then they influenced its selling price by threats, bribery, and intimidation. I saw it on the faces of the people at the auction that day and watched the result of their intended outcome play out right before my eyes. After buying it themselves, they planned to sell the diamond on the black market for what it was 'actually' worth and make a considerable profit. My father found out about it, and they killed him for it. Then they destroyed my appraisal to cement their scheme. Now, they're after me because I discovered what they did.

I was staring at her then, as you are now upon these pages
with incredulity.

"And my brother?" was all I could stammer.

"He was the one who bought the diamond. He was the
highest bidder," she declared.

Slack jawed and wide eyed, I reached over and pushed the
intercom button.

"Doris, bring in the 'Good' stuff" I said,
"and three glasses."

After giving Doris the abridged version of what I just
heard, more for my own understanding than for hers, she
asked Nina, "how did you recognize him?"

"I didn't," she answered. "I didn't know who he was at
the time. All I did was follow him out of the auction house
to his hotel that night, and to the airport the next day. It
was from his hotel registry that I confiscated his vital
information so I could track him back here to the states.
And he led me straight to you." As she said this, she
reached out and touched my hand, and with an almost
angelic face, smiled. I swallowed hard in response.

Doris sniffled and poured three more glasses of
the 'Good' stuff.

"How did . . . ?"

"What was . . .?"

"When did....?" was all that would come out of
my mouth.

"Wait a minute," I said aloud to the both of them. The
jigsaw puzzle was beginning to take shape.

"Come with me," I said as I gently but firmly grabbed
Nina's wrist and hauled her out of her chair and through

the office. Doris was close on our heels. I walked over to the basement door, threw it open, switched on the light, and walked down the stairs to the bottom with everybody in tow. The reaction that ensued when Nina laid eyes on my trussed captive was almost as bad as it was when she saw Babe for the first time. And then she went ballistic.

"You killed my father you bastard Bolshevik," she screamed as she ran across the basement to apparently scratch his eyes out. I had to physically restrain her from doing so. Although I had second thoughts at the time. I then had to literally drag her kicking and screaming, in Russian no less, back up the steps.

After several minutes of hand holding and cajoling, motherly proverbs and advice, and more of the 'Good' stuff, she calmed down. Well, down enough to have a reasonable conversation.

"What is he... what is he... doing here?" she stammered breathlessly.

"You're the one that just told me about you, the diamond, the mob and the...."

"HET...HET... no-no," she cut in, "what is he doing HERE?" she said emphatically while pointing to the basement. I was mentally writing all this off as a breakdown in communication. A language barrier; 'so-to-speak.'

The jigsaw puzzle, however, was coming together even more. But there was a large keystone missing.

"I'll tell you all about it on the way over to see my brother," I informed her.

"Doris!" I said to her as we exited the building, "hold the Fort. And if you don't hear from me in an hour, call the police. And only water, no bread!"

Chapter 17
"I've been better..."

On the way over to my brother's studio, I explained to Nina, to the best of my knowledge, what I believed was taking place. Or at least the way I had figured it out up to this moment in time. I parked behind the studio as usual, right next to my brother's car, so I knew he was inside.

"Mark!" I called out. "Mark, hey bro, where are ya'?"

"Come on in and join the party" he replied just as we walked through the studio's inner doorway.

The tableau that greeted us was straight out of the movies. My brother, beaten to a pulp, and bloodied beyond 'almost' recognition, was still conscious and sitting in a chair. Over him stood the 'Lurch' clone, hands all bloody and shredded and holding a 9-millimeter gun to my brother's head. The room had been tossed and all his valuable musical instruments were in ruin. At her first glimpse of Mr. 'Lurch,' Nina through both hands up to her mouth, inhaled sharply and took two steps backwards as though he was contagious. That reaction, coming from Nina upon seeing him, was not unexpected.

"Looking for something?" I said to Mr. 'Lurch' as I scanned the room.

"Hey to you too bro," Mark groaned.

"Shut up" said 'Lurch' to my brother.

"It speaks," I said.

At this statement, the 'Lurch' "look alike" slowly trained his gun on me. Nina started to whimper slightly as she moved ever so slowly behind me.

'Lurch' made his way over to me, wearily, and began to frisk me down. He removed my handcuffs from my belt and my Beretta from my ankle holster. During this time, I was watching my brother for any positive signs in his condition. And wouldn't you know it, he was half smirking in my direction.

When he saw my concerned expression, he just grinned and said, "I've felt better."

This, I believed. I really did.

"Why don't we all just relax, take a seat and settle down while we wait," said Mr. 'Lurch' as he motioned with his gun to the rooms empty chairs while walking around himself.

Nice of him to suggest it, I thought. So, I began strategically maneuvering Nina around the room while acquiring a seat and trying to outflank him.

"No, no, no," he said waving his gun and indicating that we all should be sitting together. We did so, begrudgingly.

"And by the way," he croaked. "Thanks for bringing HER along," indicating Nina with a point of his nose. "We've been looking for her."

Now he was starting to 'piss me off.' I turned my attention back to my brother, both out of concern and to keep my poker face intact.

"Are we waiting for anyone or anything in particular?" I asked my brother.

"Mr. Hold" volunteered Mr. 'Lurch.'

"I wasn't talking to you 'ass-wipe'" I exclaimed as I trained my attention back to our captor. Nina vocalized a soft groan as she lightly touched my forearm.

"Eh, eh, eh," said handsome, shaking his gun in a 'no-no' fashion.

I smiled in her direction and mentally thanked her as she withdrew her hand.

It then dawned on me what the henchman had just uttered.

"Mr. Hold you say. Well, now we've come full circle and we're waiting for the lynchpin, are we?" No reply.

I looked at my brother.

"Oh, where are my manners? I forgot, you two haven't been formally introduced. Mr. Mark Rivers, Miss Nina Thymins. Miss Thymins, my brother, Mark Rivers."

You've met her once before bro, you just don't remember."

At this statement, my brother looked somewhat perplexed.

"Nice to meet you, ... again?" he said, inclining his head towards her.

"Your brother is misleading you" she said, and she gave me a sideways lear.

"In Russia, at the auction. I watched you bid," she exclaimed.

"Oh," he whispered, as he closed his eyes and lowered his head.

"Anything you'd like to add to this story? You know. . . fill in the blanks?" I inquired.

"This, I'd like to hear myself," said 'Lurch' as he sat half-assed on the far end of the pool table and crossed his arms.

"I'll try to make this as short and concise as I can," said my brother as he raised his head to look at his audience.

"Oh, don't rush on my account," said 'Lurch.'

"I've got time."

The three of us just glared at him with unpleasant, independent thoughts. After a deep inspiration, and a forceful expiration while simultaneously rubbing the blood off his lips, my brother looked up and began.

"You know when I moved back home, I didn't have very much money. Heh, that's why I moved back home" he chuckled. "I had an idea for this recording studio, but I couldn't find any banks that would finance my dream. I even tried endowments for the arts and grants. After a few months, my dreams weren't looking so hopeful until a friend of a friend, you know how it goes, told me about this organization that was lending money with low interest rates. I thought to myself, why not, I'll check it out. That's when I had the pleasure of meeting 'this gentleman' and his associates" he said with the shake of his head. "I knew the whole thing was too good to be true. That it wasn't on the 'up and up'. But I had to take a chance. Everything was sailing along smoothly until about a month ago, when again this 'gentleman and his associates', and I use the term loosely, came by to pay me a visit. They said, in lieu of the 'favorable' lending terms I've enjoyed over the years, they had a small favor owed them. This 'small favor' involved a trip to Moscow to bid

on some unknown item at this auction house, purchase it and bring it back here where they would claim it and theoretically, go away. Initially, I didn't think anything looked wrong on the surface. Not until I got over there and saw what I was bidding on and how much money they had instructed me to wager. The latter, written on a piece of paper and placed in an envelope, slid under my door in the middle of the night prior to the auction. Talk about intrigue. I suspected this bunch had long arms, but I didn't know they were that long." At that comment, my brother looked at 'Lurch' who just gave him a shoulder shrug. My brother in turn, looking at me said,
"I didn't realize all this was connected until you came by the other day and told me that you had seen this gentleman and his compatriots at the record company. I then put two and two together, and realized I was dealing with the same people. And, I was being squeezed from both ends."

"But where's the diamond?" asked Nina.

"A very good question indeed Miss Thymins," commented a rugged old voice in a thick Russian accent which emanated from an elderly gentleman limping into the room. At the very sight of him, Nina had that same gut reaction that she was famous for, when confronting all the men who killed her father. I could only internally empathize with her under the current circumstances.

The puzzle pieces just kept on coming.

"Where/are/MY/manners?" said my brother slowly rising to his feet.

"I forgot, the two of you haven't met yet. Jake Rivers; Ian Hold, President of the Phoenix Music Publishing Company, and bad guy. Mr. Hold, Jake Rivers, my brother. Private Investigator and good guy."

"Sit down" snorted Hold.

My brother slowly collapsed back into his seat.

"Thanks bro. Now let me return the favor.

Mark Rivers, musician extraordinaire and cool dude, meet Ian Hold of the Bratva, the Russian mafia. And bad guy!"

The two Russians chuckled conjointly thinking all this was humorous.

"All this is very amusing, Mr. Rivers, Mr. Rivers," he said nodding respectively to us both.

"But, as Miss Thymins so eloquently put it, where's the diamond?" he asked demandingly.

"Hey! You know I'm kind of curious about that myself" I said, turning in my seat to address my brother sitting next to me, as though we were sharing a morning cup of coffee.

"How did you get it out of ol' Mother Russia?"

"Funny you should ask," he said while turning to face me, as though we were the only two people in the room.

Before I left, 'Boris Badenov' here, gave me specific instructions as how to get out of Russia with the diamond.

I had to see 'certain people', fill out certain forms for insurance companies, the **De Beers** company, Sotheby's, the government, 'yadda' 'yadda'. While I was doing all that, I got a very peculiar feeling that I was 'being played.' And I wanted to have a little…. 'backup' insurance for myself in case all of these 'well thought out plans' went South.

"Must run in the family," I said shaking his hand.
"So, I went to the president of Sotheby's and expressed my concern about traveling with such a rare commodity all by myself. They were more than happy to elaborate on the extensive security they have in place for situations just like this. Double and triple box systems, armored car transportation, armed guard escort and its own security plane to name a few. How thoughtful. So, I took them up on it. Well, in theory I did. I went through the motions, and when it was time to crate the little gem, I dropped a rock in its box wrapped in blue velvet to take its place. Nobody was the wiser, and the poor old 'sedimentary' lady had a wonderful trip to the United States snug as a bug in…. five or six crates. And then, I brought the diamond home exactly as 'Boris' here told me to. When I got home, it was just as easy to tell 'Boris' the opposite story. They were all waiting for their package to arrive on a plane a week later, and boy, were they surprised. In the meantime, 'Nothing' up my sleeves, 'pifft'…"
And he did a wonderful imitation with his hands of a magician's disappearing act.
"Bravo" I said clapping, "bravo."
In reply to my acknowledgement, he did a short waisted, seated bow.
"Well, that explains quite a bit Mr. Rivers," growled Hold as he pulled a Glock out of the waistband of his pants.
"Thank you for filling in the blanks for us.
Now, where is the diamond?"

My brother, slowly rising and nonchalantly strolling over to the right side of the pool table, placed his hands on the ledge and said,

"Ah, come on guys, can't we settle this in a less dramatic fashion. Why don't we play a good old-fashioned game of billiards, winner take all."

During his last comment, Mark looked directly into my eyes.

"Enough playing" Holt said to Mr. 'Lurch.'

"Start killing them one at a time until somebody talks." Following this directive, 'Lurch' swiveled, still sitting on the far corner of the table and pointed his gun directly at me.

"Jake!" Mark yelled as he leaned across the table right in front of me. As a single gunshot sounded in the room, I yelled to Nina, "GET DOWN" while pushing her out of her chair to the floor. I simultaneously rolled under my end of the pool table and grabbed the shotgun. Without the least bit of hesitation, I cocked the gun, rolled to and out the opposite side of the pool table our friend 'Lurch' was sitting on and dispatched him to a place only Jimmy Hoffa knows well. I quickly scanned the room for Ian, who had, naturally, disappeared during the commotion. I crawled my way to the opposite side of the pool table to my brother, who's labored breathing I could hear from this distance. When I reached him, I stretched out my arm and touched him, in the vain attempt to gather any vital sign information my subconscious thought was necessary at the moment. While doing this, my brother clasped my hand in both of his, and with a firm but gentle pressure, patted them. Looked at me and said,

"There's no place like home bro ….."

"There's… no…. pla….."

And he was gone.

During surreal moments like this, it's funny the things your mind focuses on. Right now, all I could think of was……

"Why in the name of God was my brother quoting proverbs from the Wizard of Oz to me?"

And that question kept repeating in my mind as I slowly turned around to make sure Nina was OK. Have I ever told you what a great hugger she is?

Chapter 18
Oh, No you Don't.

Two days following the death of my brother, in a third-floor private office of The Phoenix Music Publishing Company in Philadelphia PA, a weary but determined old Russian was inspecting his 'carry on' bag for any items he may have inadvertently forgot.

"Going somewhere?" a voice said from behind him.

He instinctively reached back into the bag.

"Oh please, go right ahead," I said. The term "make my day" came to mind, but instead I said, "You'll save me all the trouble of doing paperwork later, and I hate paperwork."

After hearing this, he slowly withdrew his hand from his bag.

"That's a good boy," I said as I made my way slowly towards him and fastened the handcuffs on his wrists behind his back.

"How did you find me?" he asked.

"Criminals always stay close to home," I said. "Or is it, 'always return to the scene of their crime?'
I always get those two mixed up."

In a 'not so gentle' manner, I pushed him towards the elevators.

"Come on 'Boris' I said, "the rest of your 'fractured fairy tale' mob is waiting for you in a cell not too far from here. Oh, and by the way, when you get back to Russia, tell Natasha I said 'hi'."

One of the nicer things about collaring someone in a big city like Philadelphia, is that the FBI building isn't that far away. They were extremely glad to take my guests off my hands along with all my evidence.

Extradition to Russia was a 'piece of cake.' The Kremlin was more eager to get them back to their country than we were to kick them out of ours. The Russian government may have its faults, but I will give them one thing, they sure do like to prosecute people.

And, as it turned out, besides honoring the charges The United States was referring them for, the Kremlin had a list of infractions they too were prosecuting them for as long as my arm. I'm always eager and willing to cement better relationships between people, or in this case, countries, as best I can. Chalk it up to good old American principles.

Chapter 19
Road Trip

Several weeks later, in my office, Doris was helping Nina and I prepare for our trip to Russia. Nina had a lot of loose ends to secure as well as knots that needed to be untangled pertaining to and concerning her profession, the Department of the Interior, the Museum, not to mention at De Beers and Sotheby. She also had to take care of some personal matters. In the advent of the state's prosecution of Ian Hold and company on charges from murder and extortion to fraud and theft, the state agreed to take a very small amount of time off his very large number of years in prison, if he were to divulge the whereabouts of Yuri Petroff.

And wouldn't you know it, Nina asked me to come along. Well, I couldn't say 'no.' Somebody had to keep her out of trouble.

Being a private investigator for as long as I have, you start to develop gut instincts about things. Become more 'attune' and sensitive to cosmic vibrations. At present, I was starting to feel certain 'vibes' while sitting at my desk. When I glanced up, I noticed that Doris, whose eyes were fixated on me, was holding up the office door frame with her body, or was it the other way around? She also looked as though her dog just died. With a grave air about her and doing a 'Jacob Marley' shuffle into the office, she extended her hand towards me which held an envelope.

"It's from Mark" she sobbed.

My arm, which I had extended spontaneously to meet with hers, froze in midair. I don't know how long I would have stayed in this position if it wasn't for Nina's intervention. She had the wherewithal to take the envelope, the courage to open it, and the decency to hand it to me to be read.

Hey bro!

Don't freak-out, it's only me.
I made a deal with the post office, that if I personally didn't cancel the delivery of this letter by a certain date, they were to post it.
Obviously, if you're reading this, they must have sent it. And since they sent it, I can guess things 'went south' pretty fast. I hope you're OK.
I can only imagine how you're feeling. But don't worry about me, I'm fine.
Tell Doris I said hi.
I just wanted to say, "I love you."

There IS no place like home.

PS you were right all along, Hank Aaron isn't the greatest home run hitter of all time.

Mark

The deathly silence in the room was broken only by
my mumbling.
"I don't get it. I just don't get it. Why would he do this?
I know he's trying to tell me something, but I just . .
don't . . see it.
'What gives' with all the Wizard of Oz proverbs?

And he would have gone to his grave rather than admit
Hank Aaron wasn't...."

That's when the tears started.
And Nina held me as I wept and smiled.

The De Beers and Sotheby companies were more than
happy to get their diamond back. Now they could sell it
for its real value and make respectable and honest profits.
The finder's fee Nina and I decided to split wasn't a bad
perk either. The Russian government was ecstatic. This
would remove some tarnish from their reputation and
give them an increased sense of national pride when it
was displayed at their Museum of Natural History as Yuri
Petroff would have wanted.

Epilogue

During life's quieter moments, when I reminisce about my brother, I'd like to think that his sacrifice was in payment of an old childhood debt. It doesn't compensate for his absence, but it lets me sleep better most nights. The song that we wrote together never did make it to the top 20, but it did get some very favorable reviews from the trade magazines. And as for Nina and myself? I don't have to look into her eyes anymore to see my children.
I just have to look around the living room.

As is true with all stories, once they begin, they must end. So too is it true at the end of this tale, MY story. From the resolution of my "predicament", one might ask themselves; was all the lying, cheating and deceit, as well as the loss of a loved one worth it? Not really.
You might say, it was
"All for Nothing." All but Love that is. Go figure.

131

Special thanks to the following artists and companies for their contribution of free clip art.

Stockio.com

Johnny_Automatic

About the author. .

      Joe Mannherz is a Physical Therapist by profession. Retired. He has been singing since the age of 8. From boy soprano in his church choir to tenor in his high school and later college chorus. He also plays several instruments. He's even built his own Vibraphone and Marimbas.

   He has been a member of the Barbershop Harmony Society for over 45 years; a 30-year member of the Baltimore Symphony Chorus; a member of the Handel Choir and the Concert Artists of Maryland.

    He has been the Musical Director of Harford County's "Bay Country Gentlemen" and Harrisburg's "Keystone Capital Chorus". He is currently the Artistic/ Musical Director of his jazz quintet "High Five" and the "Baltimore Vocal Jazz Ensemble."
Along with directing/music arranging/vocal coaching, he can add several stage appearances to his credit; A Funny thing happened on the way to the Forum, 1776, Man of La Mancha, Sound of Music, O'er the Ramparts, Little Mermaid, Jesus Christ Superstar, the Wizard of Oz, and Beauty and the Beast to name a few of the most recent.

Amateur Sleuth

The burning question one should be asking themselves when they finish reading this book is:

Where did Mark hide, and Jake eventually find the diamond?

By using your keen observation and deductive reasoning, you should be able to come to the same conclusion Jake did after reading Mark's letter.

If you think you know, drop me an e-mail with your solution/answer. If correct, I will enroll you as an official member of the **Jake Rivers Fan Club**. If not, and you're still curious, I'll send you a hint.

jmannherz@verizon.net

Made in the USA
Middletown, DE
17 October 2023

40848295R00083